Enjoy!

Mary Jane Atanaszek

SARA WANTS TO KNOW

by Mary Jane Stanaszek

Illustrations by Michaelin Otis

ISBN 10: 1-59298-123-2

ISBN 13: 978-1-59298-123-6

Library of Congress Control Number: 2005909739

Printed in the United States of America

First Printing: November 2005

09   08   07   06   05   6   5   4   3   2   1

Cover and interior design by John Toren

Beaver's Pond Press, Inc.
7104 Ohms Lane, Suite 216
Edina, MN 55439-2129
(952) 829-8818
www.BeaversPondPress.com

To order, visit www.BookHouseFulfillment.com or call 1-800-901-3480.
Reseller discounts available.

for Walter, Beth,

Jennifer, and Sara

Sara felt sad,
        but she didn't know why.

She had just about everything she could want.
She had a mom and a dad who loved her very much.
She lived in a nice house and went to a good school
and knew lots of kind people.

Most of all, she had her dog, Frankie.
Frankie was her best friend. They did things together all
the time. Frankie loved to chase squirrels
and birds and kids on bikes.
But best of all, he liked
just to be with Sara.

Sara didn't like feeling sad. She wanted to know
how to make that feeling go away.

She thought and thought and thought.
She thought while she was jumping rope.
She thought while she was eating dinner.

She even asked Frankie while they were
playing ball, but he didn't know.
He just looked at her and seemed sad too.

Sara decided she would ask
some wise people what they
did when they were sad.
She asked her teacher,
Miss Chang,
about feeling sad.

Miss Chang said, "I go for a walk.
I try to be quiet inside and think about
why I feel sad.
Even when I can't change anything, I
don't feel so sad anymore."

So, after school, Sara took Frankie for a walk. But Frankie kept barking at cats and cars, and she didn't feel quiet at all.

She asked Dr. Walter, their neighbor.

Dr. Walter said, "I go for a swim.
The refreshing water always helps me feel better."

Sara liked that idea.
But she had chores and homework to do, so
    there really wasn't time for swimming.

Sara still wanted to know, so she asked
Mrs. Pipestone at the library.
Mrs. Pipestone said, "I pull weeds or pick
flowers in my garden. I enjoy the
beautiful trees and listen to the birds
singing. Nature helps me feel not
so sad anymore."

On her way home, Sara looked at the trees and the flowers, but she didn't look where she was walking and stepped into a big mud puddle.

She asked her dad's friend, Mr. Osi, when he came to visit.

Mr. Osi said, "I read my holy book, the Koran. This helps me remember what's important in life. Then I don't feel so sad."

So Sara found her favorite books and sat down to read. But her friends called, and she didn't have time to read at all.

Sara still wanted to know, so she asked
her friend's grandfather, Rabbi Brad, about
feeling sad.
The Rabbi said, "If I thank God for my
blessings, I always feel better."

Sara said her prayers before she went to sleep and again the next morning.
"Oh, dear!" she said. "I always remember to say my prayers, so why do I still feel sad sometimes?"

Sara sat down with Frankie.
"Other people get sad, just like me.
Different things help them feel better.
But how do I know what works best
for me?"

Sara was feeling very, very discouraged.

Just then Frankie chased a squirrel up a
tree.

He barked and
barked.
He jumped and
jumped but
couldn't reach the
squirrel.
He ran around the
tree, then started
chasing his tail.
Finally he just sat
down with his
tongue hanging out.

He looked so funny that Sara
started to laugh.
She laughed and laughed.
"Oh, my," she said.
"Now I know what
makes me feel
better—

It's YOU,
Frankie!